The Lottery

How a question can change a life

OTHER BOOKS BY MATT RAWLINS

The Question
The Namer
The Container
The Gate & other short stories
Rediscovering Reverence

LEADERSHIP BOOKS

The Green Bench
A dialogue about Change

The Green Bench II
Ongoing dialogue about communication

Emails from Hell

The Lottery

How a question can change a life

Matt Rawlins Ph.D.

Amuzement Publications
A Green Bench Series by Matt Rawlins

Cover design by Hye-Kyung Kim

The Lottery by Matt Rawlins.
Copyright © 2004Matt Rawlins.

Library of Congress Catalog Card Number: 2001119767

Dedication

To my older brother Mark who passed away Oct 1993, from cancer. You are gone but not forgotten. In a better place but terribly missed here. Thanks for loving me.

THE BEGINNING Part 2

Mark sat at his desk in his apartment. He muttered to himself, "Who would have thought a year ago anyone would be interested in what I have to say? A kid with a couple of years of college under his belt and a knack for computers." He laughed out loud, "Ha, I didn't even listen to myself."

He looked over at the small stack of papers and pondered out loud, "I have had five publishers asking if they can publish my reflections from this last year. But there is only one lucky one and the courier to pick it up and me with it will be here soon." He stood up and walked over to the mirror and looked at himself. He knew the radical changes that had taken place inside him but they could not be seen. The only things that could be seen were the new clothes and the way he carried himself. Mark ran his hand over the soft brown leather coat, lifted his right foot and rubbed the top of his new Rockport shoe on the back of the jeans on his left leg and then did the same with the left foot. He checked the collar on his blue dress shirt as he lifted and moved his head around. Yes, there was something definitely different about him.

He walked back over to the desk and penned his last thoughts. An hour later, the introduction of the finished manuscript was done.

It's time to tell my story.

It has been a very hard year with all the pressure from the media and everyone's expectations. Only now can I begin to understand the crazy turn of events. As many of you will remember I was one of two people in the world who received The Book. Who would have thought it had the power to transform a life like mine. I wouldn't have. In fact my first thought was just to throw it away.

But then, I couldn't do that, knowing how much had been paid for it in the auction. Yet, given time, it has opened new doors and helped me see the world in ways I never dreamed possible. I guess in essence it opened my eyes up and gave me a fascination for, and understanding of myself and others. I trust it would do the same for you. The power is not in The Book, but what it has to teach. A very simple idea, but a powerful tool to help find and keep a life we all want. But that was a year ago and I am at the end of this story. Let me start from the beginning.

P.S. I have tried to stay with the actual diary of my year. Some parts have been tidied up, and slow days and weeks removed to keep the material interesting.

Mark held the manuscript in his hand for a few moments and just looked at it. "It is finished; or is it just beginning?" He smiled at the question, then slid the manuscript in a folder and sealed it. The doorbell rang and he walked over and opened the door. The man who was picking him up was right on time. Mark asked for some ID and once it was confirmed, he walked out to hand deliver to the publisher the final draft with all corrections made. Just as he was closing the door he took off his hat and threw it into the room. He wouldn't need it anymore. He closed the door and walked into a very different world.

THE BEGINNING Part 1

An enormous red banner with glittering gold letters hung across the columns in front of the Smithsonian Museum of Natural History in Washington D.C. The words on the banner simply said, "Welcome." It was the day of the auction. As the proceeds would go to the Museum, the Museum gladly agreed to host the event. One of the two books was to be sold to the highest bidder. Those who were allowed to attend needed a guarantee of 100 million dollars that could be immediately transferred into the auction account. No expense was spared in the lavish preparation.

The lottery to give away the second book was to be held at the same time. Anyone who wanted his or her name included had signed up in the last year. As there was no cost, anyone with a dream or an ounce of hope within the boundaries of the U.S. had signed up. The lottery was held at a hidden location and would be broadcast live as soon as the final price at the auction was determined.

Power and wealth flowed from those who gathered for the auction. The names read straight out of the "Who's Who of the World's Richest." The limousines began to arrive early and the wealthy strutted along the red carpet up the stairs. Men of all ages in tailored tuxedos, women of all sizes and shapes in designer dresses and enough jewels to stock all the jewelry stores in Washington D.C. flowed up the stairs, under the banner and into the entryway. The reporters lined the edges of the railings and called out questions, "What will you do with the tools discovered in The Book?" "How much will you pay for The Book?" Few answered as they walked into the building. Every once in a while a limousine drove past the red carpet to a more discreet entrance in the back.

Everyone arrived and the luxurious leather seats were full. Silence slowly settled over them all. Anticipation gathered momentum. A 17th century English clock struck six and a tall, skinny man appeared at the podium. Impeccably dressed in a black tuxedo, he welcomed the crowd, "I trust you have found your place and everything is to your liking. We would like to thank you for your interest. I know you have not come to hear me speak so we shall begin." A small Plexiglas container was carried out and inside it was a handcrafted leather book placed on a purple velvet covered stand. It was set on the table before everyone.

The tall host began, "As you all know my employer was a rather eccentric man. His last years were spent trying to find the keys that would save mankind from destroying themselves while creating hope for tomorrow. He spent his entire fortune, which was no small feat, and hired thousands of researchers from all over the world. He had a computer system built that could compile the data. No one but himself was allowed to read all of it. Historical archives were carefully examined. No page was left unturned as these researchers looked for keys to success in helping humanity move forward. The research was compiled and placed very carefully in two books. Someone here today will purchase one. The other will be given away in a lottery. How you deal with the information is up to you. Your purchase of The Book will fund research for many years to come. You only have the person from the lottery to contend with, as you will be the only two people alive to know what this book contains. For this reason I must say, we make no guarantee of the material that is in this book.

"Ladies and Gentlemen, let the bidding begin. We will start at 75 million dollars. Who will begin?"

The bidding jumped higher and was more than anyone wanted to think about before it began to slow down. In everyone's mind was the awareness of the lottery to be held at the end of the final bid. It might be that the person who won would just give The Book away. Or it might be that it could be bought from them as well.

"Are there no more bids?" Everyone held their breath. Finally the podium was struck with a small block of wood as the man stated, "Then Bidder Number 121 has purchased The Book. Thank you for your participation." The bidder slowly strutted up and grasped the Plexiglas container. He turned to look at the group as he held the container. He beamed and seemed to drink in the look everyone gave him. Finally he slowly turned and walked out of the room through a private exit followed by security guards.

• • •

The rest of the country sat before their TV sets and watched eagerly as the host of the lottery stood waiting. The different announcers were all speculating about the auction as they waited for the signal from the host that the lottery would begin. The signal was given.

"Ladies and gentleman. I have been given the signal that the auction is over and a bid has been accepted." A broad shouldered man walked out from behind a curtain with a Plexiglas container with a handcrafted leather book inside. It was identical to the other container and book. It was placed on the table before the cameras.

"Without further adieu, as I push this button it will signal the computer to randomly draw the name of the person selected." The host pushed the button and a name appeared on the screen and the host read it, "The name of the person is Mark

Stephen. Let me repeat. The name of the person is Mark Stephen. We will not give out his address until he has been contacted personally."

Every reporter and researcher in journalism kicked into high gear. They checked every Mark Stephen on record, where they lived, and began to try and find which one it might be.

• • •

The winner, Mark Stephen got the call. He had been out playing basketball at the YMCA. He walked into his apartment, threw his gym bag on the floor and hit the play button on the answering machine. The first couple of messages were old news. He pulled off his favorite Mickey Mouse shirt and 'shot' it at the laundry basket, "two points" he yelled as it dropped in. He headed for the shower. He leaned out of the bathroom at a new strange voice and heard, "you have won the lottery for The Book. Please contact us ASAP. Our number is…"

He stopped in his tracks and mumbled, "What the…?" he walked back out and hit the play button again and forwarded to the message. "This is the host of the lottery that was just held for The Book. Your name was chosen and you have won the lottery for The Book. Please contact us ASAP. Our number is…" Mark scribbled the number down that was given. He just stood there mumbling, "lottery, what lottery are they talking about? What is this Book?"

The phone rang and Mark picked the receiver up off of the Mickey Mouse base, "Hello?"

"Are you Mark Stephen?"

"Yes."

"Are you the winner of the lottery?"

"I guess so. Someone just called. Who is this?"

"I am from 20/20 and I would like to interview you. Can you please confirm that you live at…"

He froze like a deer in the headlights. Mark could hear the person on the phone calling out, "hello, hello, are you there?" Finally

Mark chirped out, "I don't want to talk to anyone," and hung up. He turned on the TV and watched as all the stations were putting his name on the screen and talking about the lottery. They were looking for him. He remembered months ago putting his name down for the lottery and The Book and then forgetting about it. He called the number and told them where he lived and they said they would be there in the morning. He quickly grabbed his towel and headed for the shower. Images of instant fame began running through his mind. His smiling picture on all the magazines covers. He looked into the mirror and saw his tall skinny frame, light brown hair and wide nose staring back and said, "Show me the money!"

Mark got out of the shower and answered the phone. He was immediately sorry. He tried to talk, but they wanted information he didn't have. Finally he just hung up on them. "I don't know anything about The Book," he mumbled. The phone didn't stop ringing for the rest of the evening. Mark finally turned off the ringer.

Mark went to his room and stood looking at his clothes. He noticed news trucks starting to show up outside. He turned the TV up loud so he could hear everything and went to his room. What should he wear? *Jeans? Basketball jersey? Dress shirt?* After fifteen minutes of putting on and then taking off clothes he was disgusted with himself. He mumbled, "I know what a girl feels like now." He finally threw on a nice pair of slacks and his only clean dress shirt. "I don't want to disappoint the ladies watching," he declared.

Within the hour reporters filled the parking lot, knocking on his door and milling around waiting for him to appear. He went out and tried talking with them but they kept pushing to get at him and after a hundred, "I don't knows," he decided he had had enough. He retreated back into his apartment, locked the door and decided not to go out as more and more people gathered. Mark turned most of the lights off and stood behind barely open blinds and watched all the people outside waiting for him. Images of being the last kid picked in every game he ever wanted to play flooded his mind. Cloaked in darkness, Mark was afraid and yet, he couldn't stop grinning.

Mark stood there for an hour and as people started to leave he decided to watch some TV and hit the bed. It was a long, sleepless night and he just finished redressing for the 10th time when the lottery representative arrived. After some pushing and shoving, he made it to Mark's door. With the representative's ID established, he then escorted Mark out the door to the waiting limousine. Mark was whisked away and before he knew it he found himself in New York before a large audience receiving the Plexiglas container with The Book inside. The flashes from the cameras almost blinded him. He grinned and held up The Book like a trophy. Flash backs of older kids throwing him into trashcans as a kid popped into his mind. He wanted them to see him now. He reached up and kissed The Book and the flashes intensified. He marched back and forth and did everything the photographers asked. It was a form of revenge and he was enjoying every second of it. It was intoxicating, like nothing he had ever experienced before.

Finally he stepped up to the podium and began, "I am honored to own this wonderful book. I feel like I have been chosen to move humanity forward. As Armstrong once said, 'One small step for man, one large step for mankind.' Granted, this is not the moon, but it certainly is unknown territory. I will talk more later. Thank you."

Accompanied by guards, Mark walked out the entrance of the Museum and down the steps. He headed towards the bank around the corner where he had asked them to set up a safe-deposit box to hold The Book. As he was trying to move through the crowds a large limousine pulled up and a man jumped out and asked Mark, "May I ask you something?"

Mark responded, "Go for it, but be quick. This is all a little nuts."

The man leaned over and whispered to Mark, "I will give you $10,000 dollars to get in this limousine with me and appear on the Today Show that is on right now."

Marks jaw dropped and the flashes from the cameras went wild. He stood for a moment and then said, "But I need a guard and I need to get it to the vault."

The man whispered again, "I will give you an extra $2,500 to bring it with you and it just so happens that I have two guards with me in the limo."

The man gently reached out for Mark's arm and said, "May I help you in?"

Mark dived into the Limo and the next thing he knew he was being interviewed on the Today Show.

When Mark was asked what he thought was in The Book he jumped right in, "I am sure it has answers to most of the problems we face today. Cancer! AIDS! Who knows? It may give us a leap forward in new areas. It could help move our country forward as the greatest civilization that has ever been. I look forward to going through the material and making it available as it seems appropriate."

The interview was finally over and it seemed the weight of The Book grew with each passing moment. They ushered him to the Limo and they took off for the bank vault. The man began, "I can confirm you on Larry King, Leno, 60 Minutes wants a slot. You name it and it is yours. You can make a good living at this. The man passed Mark a check for $12,500. Mark held it in his hands and couldn't believe it. He sat there stunned, "give me a little time to think about it."

"As you wish, but beware, public opinion and interest is rather fickle. You don't want to miss this opportunity," the man replied as he gave Mark a card and said, "Call me by tomorrow morning."

Mark took the card and nodded.

They arrived at the bank and to his utter amazement there was still a crowd mulling around. Mark got out and the guards pushed their way up the stairs to the entrance to the bank.

Mark walked into the bank and down the circular stairs into the vault. After all the noise and questions, the quietness was a relief. He looked carefully around the vault and found only one camera at the other end by the entrance. No one would be reading over his shoulder. Mark opened the Plexiglas container and held The Book. His hands trembled as he slowly opened it and looked inside. On the first page was a simple question mark.

?

All the other pages were blank.

Mark stared, his mind as blank as the pages that were before him.

That was it.

A simple question mark.

Mark mumbled, "The tool that is going to save mankind?" He laughed out loud, "I can't believe this." He carefully looked through The Book again and again to be sure there was no hidden compartment with a computer chip, no small script.

There was nothing else. That was it. His first temptation was to throw it in the trash, but that quickly passed. He took a deep breath. Once again, he was the last kid picked. The runt of the litter. The joke was on him.

Mark opened the safe-deposit box and slid The Book in. He slammed the door and placed the key in his pocket.

Mark stood there. His comments to the world ran back through his mind. *A cure for cancer? AIDS? I am going to help mankind move forward with it?*

He looked down at the red carpet on the floor. He felt nauseous. Finally he walked out of the vault and up the stairs. Reporters lurked everywhere. He waited until they were hovering around him before he announced, "I'm going to need some time to think about it. I want to make sure I understand it before I say anything more."

One of the reporters shouted, "Can you give us any idea as to what is in The Book?"

Mark replied, "I'm sorry. I will not comment any more now. As I said I will need to think about it. I will have a formal press conference in the next couple of days. I can't give you any more information as this is all rather new to me."

Mark pushed his way through them and jumped in the first cab he could find. Mark's first attempt to find a hotel quickly failed as the reporters followed him and seemed to come out of nowhere. His second and third attempts also failed. By the fourth attempt he waited in the back of the lobby by the phones and smiled. There were no reporters anywhere to be seen. He got a room and quickly went up to it. He needed time to think.

May 1

Mark paced around the room. "What do I do now?" He mumbled to himself as he paced. "I have no one to talk to. Who is going to believe me? Truth is stranger than fiction, Arrrgh!"

Mark continued to pace as time slipped by. Three steps, touch the corner of the orange flowered bed spread, turn, ten steps to the door. Turn around, twelve steps to the shuttered window. Turn, three steps to the bed. Turn, ten steps to the door. Turn…

As the pacing seemed to burn off the excess energy his mind raced ahead. In the midst of all the thoughts, his mother's words came back to him. Words he had heard over and over again as a child. "When you don't know what to do, begin to write your thoughts. Nothing will help you more than to see your thinking on paper." Pictures of his mother journaling seemed to settle his mind. She had journaled in blank books for years. If she could survive the craziness of the family, then maybe it would help him.

Mark broke out of his pacing pattern and walked over to the desk and found some paper and a pen. He sat for a moment and was stuck. "What do I write?" His mothers words echoed in his mind, "Write from your heart. Don't worry about anyone else. Just write from your heart."

I'm in a hotel room. I couldn't bear the thought of going home, as there would be reporters camped out on my lawn. There were reporters following me but I gave them the slip and found a hotel to hide in. I have nothing to say to them or anyone else.

I am the ultimate sucker. You know, one of those guys born every minute. You see them coming and say, 'Do I have a deal for you!' I must be the sucker of the century. If I could get my hands on this eccentric joker who set me up I would wring his neck. 'Years of research, supercomputers, cross checked and validated. The Book that has the wealth of human wisdom boiled down.' Boy would the world be surprised to find out there was nothing in it but a question mark. What a stupid joke! Why did I sign up for that dumb lottery? What was I thinking? How could I be so stupid?

I wonder what was in the other book? I wonder if his is the same as mine? If it is, at least I didn't pay hundreds of millions of dollars for it like the other guy. Poor sucker really got taken. I wonder what he will do?

Mark turned on the news. He tried to find whatever he could about the old man who created The Book. Anything that could give him an insight into what the old man was thinking. Was he crazy? Did he love a good joke? Time passed quickly as Mark was consumed with getting any information he could in order to know what to do next. One reporter's words seemed to ring in his ears, "After extensive research, what we do know about the creator of this book is that he was a very eccentric man who took this project very seriously."

Later

When it seemed like he could get all the news possible from the TV set he flicked it to the movie channel and sat down in the chair to think. The Riddler's words from

Batman jumped out at him, "Riddle me this…?" A thought jumped into Mark's mind. He quickly walked over to the desk and started to write.

I have to assume the eccentric old man was not crazy. That he had a reason for doing all this. As stupid as it sounds, maybe it was a riddle or a puzzle and I have to figure it out.

The only thought I have as to where to begin is to start with questions. Am I crazy to think like this? It's like trying to fix my broken glasses. You have to take them off to fix them but you can't see without them on. Can you question questions?

May 2

I have been afraid of going outside and have
been stuck in this room. What do I say? If I
lie then I am the greater fool. If I tell the
truth I am done. They say everyone gets 15
minutes of fame, but I don't want mine to
end, not now, not like this.

I was so bored I started going through all the
drawers and found a Gideon's Bible. My
childhood church came to mind and I began
to think. Here was a book of answers. No
questions, just answers. So I picked it up
and I thought, okay, what does this book
say about questions? I looked in the back
for references but there was nothing. So I
challenged myself, how far would I have to
read before I found a question in a book of
answers?

I was thinking it was going to be a long
read. That didn't scare me badly as I had a
lot of time of my hands. I got through the
first chapter and the second and was just
into the third chapter. Adam and Eve blew it

and God arrives on the scene and then I couldn't believe my eyes. I wasn't reading more than 10 minutes in the book of answers when I found a question. Adam was hiding from God and God asked, 'Where are you?'

Okay, so I have to confess. I'm intrigued. This God, who, as the old children's song goes, 'My God is so great, so strong and so mighty, there's nothing my God cannot do.' This God's first communication to Adam and Eve was to ask a question?

Okay, he knows the answer, but he asks a question.

Why did he ask a question?
Did he know something I don't know?

May 3

Mark awoke and looked around the room. The morning light reflected off the yellow walls. He rolled out of bed and sat in the green chair and looked out the window. The view from the fourth floor wasn't the greatest but he could see a little bit of the city. He sat and thought about the day ahead.

After a short while his stomach growled and images of eggs, pancakes and bacon grew in his mind. His mouth started to water at the images and he finally jumped up, shaved with the cheap razor in the bathroom and threw on his now crumbled clothes. He stood before the door, took a slow breath and opened it half expecting to see somebody there. No one was there and he headed downstairs.

He walked out of the elevator and was halfway across the lobby when a young man in a tattered suit spotted him. He got up quickly and started walking towards him. Mark tensed as the man took out a tape recorder and held it out and said, "What was in The Book?" Without waiting he asked another question, "When will you tell us about it?"

Mark tried to ignore him and made it to the restaurant. The hostess quickly seated Mark and he asked the waitress if she would please keep the reporter away from him. Mark sat in the back and enjoyed reading a paper he found on another table while he ate his sunny side up eggs, pancakes and crispy bacon. He was tempted to count how many times his name was in the paper but then decided against it as it might appear a little egotistic. He did know it was on every page he looked at.

He finished his meal and paid his bill. He walked out of the restaurant and saw a group of eager reporters trying to anticipate his movements. When they saw him they pounced and quickly surrounded him. The questions began to fly at him. "What will you do with the book?" "Will you sell it?" "Do you think it was worth the millions it raised at the auction?" Cameras were rolling, tape recorders stuck in his face and he felt smothered.

Mark pushed through them and stated, "No comment." He made it to the elevator and kept the reporters out. He almost ran to his room and closed the door behind him. He walked over and plopped down in the green chair by the window. He grabbed the paper and pencil and began to write.

I walked out of the restaurant and there was a small crowd of reporters. I pushed through them and made it safely to my room. When I walked in and closed the door behind me, it hit me. They were asking questions. That was their job. Their job was to ask questions.

I know, I have a gift for the obvious, but I never thought about it before. The role of journalism in whatever format is to be the part of society that asked questions and communicated answers to the public.

I began to think about China, Cuba or Cambodia. In these places there was no freedom to ask questions. What happened when a government or ideology controlled the capacity of those in the news business to ask questions? Everyone suffered. Truth was lost because they could not do their job. Hmmm, I hope this doesn't mean I have to

like reporters! That thought is enough to
bring me to tears.

Why do they have to ask me questions?
Why can't they just leave me alone?

May 4

The maintenance man knocked and Mark slowly opened the door. Mark pointed out the ceiling light that was out and sat down in the green chair. The maintenance man carried his aluminum ladder over and unfolded it. He walked up it and quickly replaced the light bulb. He came down the ladder and asked, "Anything else?"

Mark replied, "No."

The man unfolded his ladder and Mark sat down at the small desk to ponder an idea that was forming in his head.

I have been sitting in my room and thinking. It seems to me that asking questions is like the rungs on a ladder. They have the capacity to move you up or down. It's funny, it seems that I have asked questions all my life and never thought about questions or where the questions you asked were taking you. It's like walking and never thinking about walking, or breathing and never thinking about breathing. No, it's different. I realize I have stopped asking questions. Thankfully, it is not the same for a person when they stop breathing and when they stop asking questions.

Or is it?

I was thinking about the question I found in Gideon's Bible. God asked Adam 'Where are you?' Could this be the start of any process? Obviously it was not a geographical question. The place was not important. As I was thinking about this I was thinking about playing soccer when I was a child. One day our coach was trying to help us. He put us in our positions and then would start a game. He told us when he blew the whistle to freeze. I can remember running towards the ball and then the coach would blow the whistle. He would then ask us, 'Where are you?' All of us would be out of position. He would put us back in position and then start again. Soon the whistle would blow and I would look around and see I was out of position. I can remember his training us to always be aware of where we we're at. I wonder if that is what God meant? In this world it is easy to be consumed with pursuing something or running from something and to forget where we are.

So, where am I?
   I am trapped in a hotel room, angry, ashamed, hiding from who knows what.

Later that Day

Mark sat in the hotel room the rest of the morning and most of the afternoon. When he could bear it no longer he walked out the door and headed down the hallway to the elevator. He left the elevator and was no more than fifteen steps into the lobby before he was encircled by a large group of reporters. It was like a feeding frenzy and he was the meal.

Mark turned around and walked straight back to the elevator. He arrived at his floor and walked down the hallway. He made it into his room and closed the door behind him.

He walked over and picked up the phone and called his work place, "I'm stuck in a hotel and I'm trying to get to work but I can't make it."

His boss replied, "Don't worry about it Mark. I have an idea to present to you. Just come see me as soon as you can."

Mark sat down in the now familiar green chair.

I'm in forced seclusion and this gives me more time to think than I have had in years. So I continue to ask the question that I finished off with. Where am I?

I know the obvious answer is that I'm caged in a hotel room. But I think it's more important to ask what is going on inside of me? I have been thinking about the reporters and why I am hiding from them.

Hmmm, I guess I'm not hiding from them. I'm hiding from myself. They provoke me and I don't have an answer.

Hmmm, I have an answer but I don't want to answer them. I could answer them easily. I could say, 'it was a stupid question mark, that's all'.

I'm afraid they will think I'm the fool. This eccentric old man set me up. I was supposed to have won something of great value and it was a stupid question mark. They wouldn't believe me, would they?

I feel like I'm back in school. I am supposed to know things I don't know. There must be something wrong with me. Stupid lottery. Stupid me. What a fool I am.

Hmmm, it's funny how I feel less a man if I don't know the answer. When that happens I assume there is something wrong with me. Who told me I have to know all things? Where did I pick up that stupid idea? Funny, I never thought to question those things before. I just react. Like I am now.

Why do I have to be the fool?
Who says I am the fool?
Who says I have to know everything?

May 5

Mark let the manager into his room and paid his bill. Because he had no luggage he went down the back stairs and out into the street. The sidewalk was crowded so Mark blended in and began to walk as quickly as possible away from the hotel. After walking for 15 minutes he found a cab and made it to his brother's house. He paid the driver and went inside.

His brother began, "There he is. The man of the hour, famous and yet, the mystery man that everyone wants to find."

Mark shook his head and held us his hands, "Listen, this whole Book thing is messing with my head. I hope you don't mind if I don't tell you about it for a while. Trust me when I say it is not simple or clear as it might appear. I need to try and figure this thing out."

Mark's brother laughed and declared, "No skin off my back. You're always welcome here. If it ain't safe with the family, I don't know where it can be. You look like you need a change of clothes as well. Find whatever you want in my closet." He had a sparkle in his eyes, "You can pay me back later. We can settle it after you make your first million."

• • •

The kids rushed into Mark's room in the morning and jumped on his bed. Mark was suddenly awake and hugged them all. It was then that the questions began, "How long will you stay with us?" "What did you win?" "Why are you staying with us? Are you moving in with us?" "Aren't those Dad's clothes on the chair?" "Where's your car?" "Why aren't you at work?" Mark answered each question and the kids were finally dragged off to get ready for school.

I am too tired to write much. I just have one thought before I start the day. Kids ask so many questions. I never realized how many they ask. It is like questions are hardwired into their minds.

• • •

After school, the kids came straight home and in between jumping on the trampoline, the questions continued. "Why did the man give you a Book and why did he sell a Book?" "What is the other man going to do with his copy?" "Did you talk with that man?" "Where is he?" The Book soon grew old to them as they seemed easily bored with books but the questions continued as the afternoon rolled on.

I haven't listened to kids before. I am dumbfounded by how many questions they ask. This afternoon, after school, I took my niece, Aimee for a walk and she asked questions the whole time. "Do we have to eat to live?" "When are you going to get married and have kids?" "Why is the sky blue?"

I t seems it is the language of children. They are not embarrassed. They are fearless. They are not concerned that they will be seen as stupid if they ask a question. They seem to enjoy not knowing, as if that makes life more interesting. They learn one of the most difficult things any human can learn, a language, and all by asking questions and being unembarrassed about not knowing. Maybe they know something I don't know.

Why did God ask a question? Was he modeling something for us?

What would happen if I started to ask questions? I'm already asking questions so I can't mean that? Hmmm, what would happen if I gave myself freedom not to know everything?

I'm going to work to talk with my boss and see what happens.

May 6

Mark borrowed his sister-in-law's van and drove to work. He parked and walked in the back door. He found his boss's office and was welcomed in.

"Sorry about missing work. I have had to hide for a while and I haven't been able to make it in."

"No problem at all. I realize it's a real challenge with all the reporters after you. I mean they have been calling here every day to try and get you. Why not use it for our benefit?" The boss reached into a drawer in the desk and pulled out a black baseball hat and handed it to Mark.

Mark took the hat and saw the company name on it. The boss continued, "I have a proposition for you. I will pay you your monthly salary if you wear this hat when you talk with the media. That's all I ask. I get the name of the company out there and you get a paid vacation for a year. What do you think?"

Mark put the hat on, "I wear this hat when I talk with the media and you'll pay me? No software, database or networking questions for a year?" Mark reached out and shook his boss's hand, "It's a deal. It's the first break I've had in a while. I'll do it. It'll give me some freedom to research The Book."

"Great, I am pleased to have you as a new member of the marketing team."

Mark made it back to his brother's house. Reporters were lined up outside. Mark made it into the house without too much hassle and told his brother and sister-in-law the story about work. His brother laughed, "Don't forget you owe me!"

"Don't worry. I won't forget." Mark pointed at the reporters on the lawn and said, "It looks like they have found me again. I think I'll head home tomorrow. You don't need them bugging you." Mark handed the safe deposit key to his brother and whispered, "Watch over this for me will ya? If something happens to me you can do what you want with The Book."

His brother gave him a stern look and said, "Yeah, sure. Just take care of yourself."

My boss offered me a marketing position. I wear the hat when I talk with the media and I get paid. I was stunned. I took the hat and walked out. I have a year's paid vacation. I can do anything I want. Hmmm, what's the best question to ask myself? How can I use this time? It's the first time I have not had others' expectations to dictate what I should do with my life. I don't know what I want. Maybe a key part of this time is to discover what I want from my life.

I have never thought like this before. Thinking about my life and which question to ask is such a radical new idea. So much to think about, at least I'll have some time to do some thinking.

I listened to my brother ask the kids a question. He asked them, 'which vegetable do you want? Carrots or Corn? He gave them a choice but they had to have a vegetable. I have heard parents ask, 'Do you want a vegetable and the kids say, 'No'. Then they had a fight. I never thought of my brother being that smart. The question validated their ability to choose but also gave them clarity about what choice they did have.

Later that night

Mark did the dishes and talked with his sister-in-law as she sat and relaxed for a few brief moments. He asked, "Has anyone ever asked you a question that changed your life?"

"Funny you should ask. I was just thinking about it this morning as I saw you with the kids. When I was 21 years old. I realized I was an adult and I could have children. All I could think about was the pain of my own childhood and how difficult it was growing up. The pain was strong. I didn't want to inflict it on children as it had been inflicted on me. I went to the doctor and asked to be sterilized. As this was no small decision, I had several interviews with different specialists and counselors."

Mark turned the water off and came over and sat down at the table, "You were going to have yourself sterilized?"

His sister-in-law nodded, "Yeah, I know. It is a scary thought now. I was down to the night before the operation and a psychologist came in and took my hand and asked one question, "How can you know for sure that this is what you want?"

"I couldn't answer him. For the first time I felt hope that I might not hurt those I gave life to. My supposed certainty was shaken by the right question. It was the right question that brought me to my senses."

As if on cue, the youngest child Markie, his namesake, ran into the kitchen and Mark just stared at him. Markie's need was quickly met and he ran off to play. Mark turned to finish the dishes and hide the tears that seemed to have a will of their own. Markie was only one question away from not being born.

I watched the kids this evening. A question by a psychologist made possible their place in this world. The right question gave them the opportunity to be here. The amazing power of a question. I hugged them tonight as they went to bed in a way I never have before.

What questions should I ask that will make space for me?
What questions should I ask that will make space for others?

In thinking of the power of a question this leads me to think, 'What if I change the question I ask myself?'

Right now I'm asking, 'What will everyone think of me?' As a result I'm hiding from the reporters. That question reveals I am afraid of what people will think. My fear is actually calling forth the question. The question I ask reveals as much about me as the answer I give. What if I ask myself the question, 'How can I benefit from this?'

Hmmm, I never thought about this before. If I change the question, it changes what I'm looking for.

May 7

I'm back to the question, 'Where are you?'
Surely God knew the best way to help us.
Why a question? Why this question? Such
a simple question is gnawing away at me. I
hear my story on the news. I read the paper
as they write or should I say speculate on
what was in The Book. They don't know
where I am. The first question I discover is
driving everyone nuts. Including myself.

What does this question say about God?
     A God who cares about us and where
we are?
     A God who wants us to care about
ourselves and to know where we are?

I have also been thinking through the questions I ask myself. Changing the question
from 'What will the world think of me?' to
'How can I benefit from this?' has changed
the way I feel about it all. Don't get me
wrong, I am not ready to go out and spill
the beans. But I am not nearly as afraid of
it all when I change the question. The hard

part of changing the questions I ask is that
I must be willing to change myself.

May 8

Mark had set up a meeting with the media and stood before them at the Museum where the auction had been held. He positioned himself behind the wooden podium with his black baseball hat on and began to read his prepared statement, "I know you are very interested in The Book and I can appreciate your interest. I must confess it is not as clear as I would have hoped. It is stated in a rather unusual way and I have decided to take a year to study it. I will make a full disclosure at the end of the year. I am afraid I will not be able to answer your questions, as I don't have any answers at this time. I will keep you posted periodically over this next year."

Mark stepped from behind the podium in the midst of all the questions being yelled at him and walked through the curtains into a back room.

Well, I did it. The Museum was glad to help so I held a press conference there. I had on my baseball cap with my company name on it. I wanted them to see that cap, as I want my year off.

I pity the poor people who wait a year for all this wisdom... Then it will be their turn to play the fool.

How will they feel when they see the question mark?

May 15

Days passed as Mark settled into his
newfound fame. On Monday he met with
officials from the lottery at the Museum to
clear up some paperwork. He walked out
the back door of the Museum and looked
around. There were people everywhere,
but no reporters rushed towards him. The
day was bright and the sun warm. A cold
breeze added to its beauty. Mark slowed
down and decided to enjoy it. He strolled
down the sidewalk towards a crosswalk
and gazed at the people swarming past. He
stopped at the crosswalk and waited for
the signal.

Mark noticed a girl coming the opposite
way and he couldn't keep his eyes off her.
She had short brown hair, large smiling
eyes, long legs and a confidence that de-
manded attention. This was better than the
weather by a long shot. The girl was looking around like she was lost and moving
towards him. She stopped right next to
him and turned to him and asked, "Do you

know where the Institute for Business Leaders is? It is supposed to be close to here but I can't seem to find it."

Mark smiled and replied, "Yeah, as a matter of fact I do. I know one of the guys who works there. Come on, I'll show you. It's just around the corner."

After a couple of steps she stopped and looked at Mark and asked, "You look familiar. What do you do?"

"Well, you probably recognize me from the lottery for The Book. I won it. I guess I've been on a few magazine covers and in the news."

"That was you! I would love to learn more about it. Can we have a meal together?" She smiled innocently as she asked the question.

Mark returned the smile and stated, "I would be glad to have a meal with you but I must warn you, I won't tell you what is in The Book. That is a secret for a while."

A look of disappointment came over her face before she declared, "That's okay.

When can we meet?"

A time and place was set and Mark walked her to the institute and then left.

I met this girl today - Lynne. She was stunning and yet interested in me. Maybe I should say interested in me as the winner of The Book. I will have dinner this Friday with her.

I walked to the park and spent the afternoon listening to myself. That sounds funny but I never realized how many questions I ask myself, particularly when confronted with issues dealing with girls and relationships. As I listened to myself, I realized that the questions I ask are more like feelings felt than real questions. That sounds so weird for a computer analyst to talk like this, but anyway, they felt like this:

Why would anyone like that be interested in me?
When is this relationship going to go bad?
What if it doesn't work out and I get dumped?

These are bad questions and will stop me even before I start. They're built on the wrong ideas. Ideas that will not let me get what I want. The idea pushing the first question is that somebody who is beautiful will not be attracted to me; I am ugly. When is this going to go bad is built on the idea that everything will go bad and is just a question of timing. The last question is built on fear. That is a terrible basis for any relationship.

These questions create doubt and I freeze up. I don't ask what am I looking for or anything like that.

Man this question thing sure can get personal. I have to expose my soul, fears and all, to try and get to the bottom of this. I'm not sure how I'm going to write this out if I publish it. Do other people think this way? Hmmm, the question forces an extreme Yes or No. Either people do or they don't think this way. What I mean is, how is this similar to what others think?

What areas are important to me in a relationship?
How can I find out what interests her?
       I can answer that right now? Ask good questions.

What is needed to make a relationship reach its full potential?

May 17

Mark picked up the ringing phone at home. He had changed his phone number to an unlisted number and few people would know it. It was an old friend, Tim, who had called Mark's mom and gotten the number. He said it was important they meet. The time was set for 11:00 that morning at Billy's Food and Billiards where they used to hang out.

They found a booth in the back and sat down. Mark looked at Tim and declared, "You shaved your head, from dreads to this shiny head thing. What in the world made you do that?"

Tim ran his hand over his head, "It has been a while since you've seen me. I did this a year ago and it drives the women crazy. Besides, I was tired of the dreads and I needed a change. Also writing for a business journal does require certain, hmmm, let's say, an appearance that doesn't scare people away."

Mark mumbled, "That is a change. There is no doubt about that."

"There have been a lot of changes in the last year for both of us," Tim hesitated and then continued, "I just heard over the line that the guy who bought The Book has disappeared. No one knows where he is or what has happened to him. There is speculation that he was murdered, but no one knows. I just thought I better tell you cause you are the only one who has The Book."

Mark sat quietly for a few moments, "I have been wondering about that guy. And I was even wondering what someone would do to me to get The Book. You may be the only person I can trust. I know you are a journalist, I have read your articles in the Leadership and Organizational Journal and I like what you write. Will you track with me over this next year and if anything happens to me, write about our time and make sure all the details of what has happened to me are out in the open? All I ask is that you don't publish anything until the year is up."

Tim pulled out a small recorder and responded, "You have my word. A year is a long time and I don't want to forget our conversations."

Mark nodded, "Fair enough. Just don't ask what is in The Book. I'm not ready to go there yet. But you'll be the first to know. I just need someone to talk with and keep me posted on what's happening."

"Anything I can do to help my friend and get the inside scoop of the year." Tim smiled and winked, "No questions on The Book huh? Okay, where do we go from here."

"The Book was in a, uh, coded form. It seems the old bird was a little more eccentric than people thought. I've given myself a year to work with it and see what I can get from it. At the end of the year I'm going public. It's still too early to know much but I have a start on some ideas. Let's meet again in a month. I'll know more then. On a side note, if something does happen to me, my brother will know where the small key is to the safe-deposit box. He can do what he wants with The Book. I'll tell him to work with you."

Tim reached over and turned off the recorder. "I will keep you posted on any news coming in, and you won't talk with anyone else about this? Agreed?"

Mark nodded and they shook hands. He pointed to the pool table and said, "What do you think? Still think you can beat me?"

Tim smiled, "Rack'em up, pal. I can't remember the last time I lost to your sorry little butt."

The guy who bought The Book is missing. I don't blame him. If I spent all that money I would disappear myself. Should I be afraid? If something happened to him, what is to stop something from happening to me?

Hmmm, maybe a better question is, "Do I need to be careful and protect myself?"

I have given the key to my brother. He said he would help out if something happened to me. He is one of the only people in the world I would trust my life with.

May 18

Mark reached over and picked up the
receiver off his Mickey Mouse phone,
"Hello."

An old friend's voice replied, "Hey, you
got any time for an old friend that's in your
part of town? I have heard about all this
stuff going down and I wanted to hear it
from the horse's mouth."

Mark laughed out loud, "It has been a long
time, way too long. Let's get together. I
would love to see you."

The old friend asked, "Where do you live?
I will be there in an hour."

"Where are you at?" Mark asked before
giving directions to his house. He then
hung up, sat down and mumbled the
words again, "Where are you? I needed to
know where he was at."

I could barely give an old friend directions as the question rang in my mind. I could not tell him how to get to my house unless I knew where he was. Knowing where you are is vital to where you are going. In fact you can't separate the two ideas. You can't know where you are going until you know where you are. That is why God asked Adam the question. He wanted Adam to know where he was so that he could then help him know where to go.

Also, as I ponder this next year, I have been struck by the thought that I am going to live some questions. That sounds funny. Let me try and explain what I understand that to be. A key question for me is who am I?

I have a kernel of an idea but it is constantly growing and revealing new areas that I hadn't seen before. I carry the question as it allows me to constantly be aware of seeing myself in different ways.

I am struggling now, as I am not sure what the kernel is that will not change. A seed will always produce its kind. What is the DNA of the identity in me that will never change and yet always be revealing new

68

aspects of itself? Another question I sense I will carry throughout my life is, What do I want from this life?

It seems to me that carrying questions is the truest form of education. I enter a quest to find more about myself. Not knowing, having a question burn inside me, is challenging and exciting. This is a part of what I saw earlier, that it is okay not to know. This is the excitement of being childlike again. What part do questions play in our world? I guess I'm finding out.

Einstein must have felt this way when he wrote, "The important thing is not to stop questioning. Curiosity has its own reason for existing. One cannot help but be in awe when he contemplates the mysteries of eternity, of life, of the marvelous structure of reality. It is enough if one tries merely to comprehend a little of this mystery every day. Never lose a holy curiosity."

Where am I curious?
How can I create more curiosity in my life?

May 19

Mark met Lynne at an Italian restaurant. She was wearing long black pants and a red and blue sweater. They sat down and Mark began, "What do you do for fun?"

Lynne replied, "I love to travel and camp. Last summer I went all over Europe. It was a blast."

"What was your favorite thing about it?"

"I love the history. Museums and old castles and buildings, they were there long before America was born. It is so rich in history and has so much to tell us."

Mark spent the evening asking questions. "Where did you find out about that?" "Did you like that?" How long did that take?" "Were you safe?" "When did you start to hear about that?"

Finally Lynne replied, "You ask a lot of questions. I have never had a guy ask me so many questions."

They talked some more and finally Mark stood up to leave. They walked to the counter and Mark paid the bill, then walked her home. She gave him her card and said, "I would love to see you some more. Call me, please."

Mark took the card with a smile and walked slowly home. He spent the next several days wrestling with what was going on in him and in the relationship.

I realize people and now particularly this girl, fascinate me. It is like writing a living software code that has the capacity to change depending on each new situation. The key code to write is linked to the questions that are asked.

As I said, this girl has really stirred me. The dinner was great. I realize that asking a good question is only a piece of a bigger puzzle. If you don't want an answer, then you won't ask a question.

Hmmm, it seems to me a question and tension is linked together. I have assumed that tension is bad, so I don't ask questions. If I think tension is good then I will be free to ask questions that create tension or allow the tension I feel to provoke a question. The question has the capacity to pull me towards a deeper relationship if I let it. My attraction to her creates a tension in me to ask questions.

There is tension in me, so what is the question?
Why is she attracted to me? That is the only thing that comes to my mind.

June 3

Mark woke and dressed quickly. He wanted to get to the library and get his hands on anything he could that might help him. He tried to do his own research so as not to give anything. He made it to the library just as it was opening and walked up to the rather large women tending the desk. She peered up at him over her black reading glasses and Mark asked, "Can you help me find some books?"

"Yes, what were you looking for?" she replied.

"I, um, am looking for books on questions."

"Questions? Can you give me more information?"

"Well, I am interested in questions. I don't know much more than that," Mark stated sheepishly.

"Questions! Questions! Let me see. Not much to go on," the Librarian stated as she looked up at Mark over her glasses.

"Tell me about it," Mark muttered.

The Librarian walked to the computer and began her search. She stood there typing something and then waiting. Typing something else and waiting some more. Mark walked over to the magazines and saw his picture on the cover of several of them. He smiled as he saw his hat included in the picture. He decided to count and found his picture on seven different magazines. He walked back over to the Librarian after a while and she turned to Mark and stated, "We don't have any books on questions. There are a few obscure books out there but we don't keep them."

Just as she was turning to go back to her desk Mark asked, "Why?"

The Librarian turned on her heels and glared over her glasses at Mark and declared, "Do you know how many people look for books on questions? None. Zero. Nada. No one. Fifteen years here and not once has a person asked." With the last statement she held up one finger and shook her head. "We carry what works for the greatest number of people and cannot stock books on every idea that is out there." With that she turned and stormed back to her desk.

I went to the Library this morning. I realized I couldn't do it on my own. I asked the Librarian to help me. In the end she stated the Library didn't have anything. I looked at her and asked, "Why?"

She looked back at me and almost slapped me. She gave a strong response and then left me alone. I walked out of the library and down the steps and reflected. 'Why' is not a good question most of the time. When you ask 'Why' it implies that something is wrong with the motive. It seems to carry with it an accusation. I think of questions:

Why did you do that?
　　There is a silent 'you should have known better' hidden in the question.

Why did you fail the test?
　　You hear a silent 'what's wrong with you?' in the question.

Why did you come?
    You hear a silent; 'you are not wanted' in the question.

When I asked the Librarian 'Why', she heard a silent, 'you are incompetent' in the question and got defensive. My question was more an accusation than a question. I know that this is not always the case, but I am going to have to be more careful.

Why did I ask why?

June 8

Mark walked with Tim around the park. They walked past an old man talking with a young man on a green bench and finally spotted a green bench to sit at. "Do you mind if I think out loud?" Mark asked.

"Go for it," Tim replied.

"I am thinking about questions and tension. I am thinking about this girl I'm going out with and my mind is muddled. Tension and asking a question are linked. It is as if tension births questions, so in one sense you can't have one without the other. Does that sound right?"

"It sounds right. I would think all communication is a result of some form of tension we sense in us or others."

"Okay, so I'm really interested in this girl. But I find myself asking, 'Why should she be interested in me?'"

Tim pondered out loud, "That's normal. Girls can be so… bizarre, you are never sure if or even why they are interested in you."

"Okay, but my assumption is that she shouldn't like me. That comes from somewhere, but where?"

"Oh, I get it. You're doing a psychobabble thing. Trying to figure it out. I don't think I can be much help. But if you were to ask me it's simply because you're a computer geek, you know a nerd. Just deal with it."

Mark stood up and started to walk as Tim joined him. Tim asked, "You don't want to talk about The Book?"

Mark looked over at him, "Your wisdom has overwhelmed me. I need to figure this thing out and you're not much help."

They continued walking as Tim replied, "Well then, some people have to get to work. Of course that's not you, but it does include me. Call me when you figure it out."

"I will call you. Thanks for the help," Mark replied as he continued the walk around the lake.

Why should she like me? It's a why question, so it's not the best question, but I have asked it and I will try and answer it. The assumption is that I am not likeable. That is a belief I have formed over the years. I can't figure girls out. They don't like me. I crash and burn. I must not be likable and that is all there is to it.

Hmmm, questions can reveal beliefs we have. Looking at the beliefs goes below the surface. In this case, it is the belief that I am not likable that causes the question of 'Why should she like me?'

June 16

Mark rolled out of bed and stumbled down the hall. He made it through the bathroom doorway and put his hands on the sink and took a deep breath and looked at himself in the mirror. He mumbled out loud, "What am I doing?" The question hung in the air and Mark reflected on it.

He walked over and pulled a dictionary off the shelf. He looked up the word *doubt* and read part of the definition out loud, "to be uncertain or unconvinced about, to be wavering or undecided in opinion or belief." As he got ready for the day he thought about doubt and how it might be linked to asking questions. Before he headed out for more reading he wrote down his thoughts.

I realize that for me to ask questions I must be able to doubt what I know. The freedom to doubt is the beginning of the capacity to question and learn. I think back on these past weeks, and I see my insecurity. When I am uncertain or not clear about what I believe or what I think I should know, I get insecure.

Hmmm, my security is based on being certain and sure about what I know.

Yet, if I'm sure and certain about everything I don't feel a need to learn anything and I stop growing and asking questions. This seems like certain death.

I'm going to have to wrestle with this more as an important piece of asking questions is a security in your self.

I must be able to doubt and be secure or I can't ask questions.

Hmmm, I doubt I'm right about this.

June 18

Mark checked his email later that day and found there were hundreds of emails waiting for him. There was now over 2,000 that he had not even opened. He also found someone was trying to break into the server and access his files. He checked the firewall and it seemed intact. There was no limit for what people would try to do to find out about The Book.

There is a cost to all this publicity. I wish I could choose when and how people would have access to my life. All this 'fame' stuff is highly over rated. But I have to be careful as it has given me a year to explore, and all I have to do is wear the company cap. That is a small price to pay.

June 23

Several dates came and went and both Mark and Lynne found themselves enjoying their time together.

Lynne began, "You know, I have been thinking about our time together. I have never talked so much in my whole life. I didn't even realize how much I learned about Europe until you started to ask me questions."

"Yeah, questions are pretty cool. I have been studying them," Mark replied.

"Studying questions? Are you nuts? No one studies questions, everyone studies answers."

"Not everyone," Mark responded.

"Okay, tell me about questions. What are you learning about them now?" Lynne asked.

"Well, this is rather awkward because I am thinking about feelings and how they are linked to questions."

"What do you mean, awkward?"

"Yeah, see that's a good question but it requires me to be more honest than I want to be. I find being honest includes my feelings, and that's hard. Let me see how I do.

Mark took a breath, "I find myself attracted to you. These are feelings that I don't want to expose."

"Oh, I see what you mean," Lynne responded, smiling.

Mark continued, "I will try and explain myself without too much self exposure. In order to ask better questions or listen to your questions I have to be willing to know where my feelings are at. Feelings strongly influence questions."

"I thought that was obvious," Lynne stated.

"Maybe for a girl it is. But for me it's not. Let me give you an example. If I just say I'm attracted to you and don't think anymore about the feeling, then I just react to a feeling. But if I'm more aware of the feeling, attracted could actually be, curious, or interested, or aroused, or lustful, or even obsessed."

"Obsessed?" Lynne said as she recoiled in mock fear.

Mark raised his hand and stated, "I'm not saying I'm obsessed with you. Just curious."

"Curious? I think more interested, or even aroused," Lynne declared.

"Let me take myself out of this conversation. The exact feeling will have to stay in the background for a while. As it relates to questions, if I just think in terms of labeling them as good or bad feelings, then it's like thinking in black and white. But if I allow there to be different aspects or intensity of feelings with levels and all, then it's like adding color and it opens up a new world of knowing and asking better questions."

"So if feelings aren't good or bad, what are they?"

Mark reflected for a moment and replied, "All feelings are important, the key is how I respond to them? The importance of a feeling or an emotion isn't measured by how pleasant it is to experience, but only by what it's intended to produce. How does that sound?"

"That's pretty analytical," Lynne hesitated and then continued, "So your being aroused by me is not good or bad. It depends on what you do with it?"

"Yeah, my curiosity in you is not automatically good or bad. It is key in the sense of what I do with it. I can ask better questions," Mark hesitated and then said with emphasis, "or run for my life."

"Well," Lynne asked, "What are you going to do?"

"Usually I would run. But I can see that it might not be the most effective way of dealing with you or even myself. I guess we will just have to wait and see. Anyway,

I need someone to practice asking questions on."

Lynne leaned forward, "Give me the best question you got."

Mark leaned forward and asked, "What are your feelings for me?"

At that moment a reporter walked up and asked, "Are you Mark Stephen? Can I ask you a few questions?"

Lynne stood up and grabbed Mark's hand and said to the reporter, "I am sorry. He is not available right now for interviews." She turned to Mark and said with a smile, "Come on, let's go. I think we have had enough questions for now."

I am continuing to date Lynne. She is great and seems to be more interested in me than The Book.

As I continue to think about all this I realize how important emotions are. I wrote earlier about how beliefs birth questions. I realize there are feelings attached to those beliefs. It is only as I understand the feelings that I can understand the beliefs.

Feelings reveal where I'm at. They reveal the answers to questions I answered earlier in my life that have formed who I am and where I am today.

The more I can differentiate between the emotions, the more I am able to understand what is going on in others and me. The more I understand what is going on inside of others and me, the richer life I can live. Like playing with only eight keys on a piano or playing with all the keys. Using the full keyboard gives me a much richer, fuller life.

If I only have a feeling described as love or hate in my vocabulary, then the relationship can be only one or the other. But if I added different aspects of emotions to the relationship then I could understand the relationship much better.

> I'm fascinated by you.
> I'm frustrated with you.
> I'm disappointed with you.
> I'm aroused by you.
> I'm nervous around you.
> I'm angry with you.

The clearer the distinction in emotions, the easier it is to understand and deal with the relationship. Knowing that you feel "bad" gives you almost no useful information about what is going on to make you feel that way, or what to do to change your situation. On the other hand, knowing precisely which emotion you are feeling provides you immediately with useful feedback. I know where I am.

I guess in its simplest form, you have to be comfortable with emotions in order to be comfortable with questions.

Where am I?
What do these feelings reveal about me?

July 28

Mark walked into Billy's. He slid into the booth with Tim and noticed the recorder was already on the table. Mark began, "Any news on the other Book or the guy's disappearance?"

Tim replied, "No. Speculation still, but it is the same old stuff. Maybe he was murdered, maybe he killed himself or he just disappeared. "

"Any sense of whether anyone wants to come after me? I mean if the other guy is gone, I am the only one who has The Book?"

"I don't know. It's interesting that he's disappeared and you have the only Book. It seems likely that many people would want what you have." Tim deliberated, "How is The Book reading going? Do you want to let me in on it in case anything happens to you?

Mark smiled, "It's going, and I'm not ready yet to open that door. Anyway, as you know I have been thinking about questions lately. What questions do you find you must ask in your profession?"

"A question that is always in the back of my mind is, 'What are the facts?' That is a key element of everything I write about. What can be verified?"

"You ever cover any police stories? What questions are they asking?"

"I used to in my earlier days," Tim replied, "They need the facts but they are also aware of motive. They are asking themselves 'Why?' If they get the 'why, they understand the crime."

"That's interesting… You got any contacts in Seattle? I want to spend a couple of days there and visit some managers and maybe even a couple of lawyers."

Tim opened his black palm pilot and pulled out his stylus. He began to tap on the screen for a couple of minutes. "I do have some contacts you can talk with. There is still a lot of hype out there about

The Book. You've seen the cover of People magazine; you're on it with the other guy. They say you both are being rather elusive. But that keeps them interested. Be sure and mention my name when you meet with these people as it is good for me to be linked to you and what you're up to."

Mark wrote down the names and put the paper in his pocket, "I don't have a lot to say right now. I am not being elusive by choice. Did anyone ever teach you how to ask questions?"

Tim smiled, "Nope. I've had to learn to ask questions or get my head chewed off by the editor for missing key pieces in the story. You learn or you die."

Mark began, "Let me try one more idea. Look around the room and find everything that is yellow."

Tim looked around the room, "Okay."

"Now, close your eyes." Tim closed his eyes and Mark continued, "With your eyes closed, tell me where all the blue things are."

Tim laughed out loud, "I know you are wearing blue jeans, and off the top of my head that is all I can think of. What's with the little play on words?"

Mark replied, "It's not a play on words. It's a matter of focus. When you are looking for one thing you don't look for other things. Questions create a focus and because of the focus of the questions we don't see other things that might be important. The questions we ask set up what we find."

Tim sat quietly and looked around the room. Finally he said, "I see some blue on the billiard balls?"

Mark got up and walked over to grab a cue. "Seems like I cleaned your clock last time. You want to try your luck?"

"Pure and simple luck. I have been waiting for the chance. Bring it on."

It seems each profession may have certain questions that are emphasized. I guess it depends upon what you're looking for. As I write this I realize it ties into what I wrote about earlier. The focus or in this case, profession, has a particular emphasis that is important.

On a side note I find myself fascinated with understanding people in ways I never thought possible. I thought technology was exciting as you got inside and began to understand what it could do. I thought people were boring compared to technology, but I must confess that is all changing. Now, I can see that people are far richer and more complex, like a type of self-writing software program.

September 3

Mark walked into a hotel in Seattle and told the reporters following him, 'I have nothing to say that is new." He checked in and found his room. He put his clothes in the drawers, as was his custom. It made it feel more like a home to him. He pulled back the curtains and saw the Space Needle not too far away. He watched the rain and wind beat against the window. Finally he reached over and picked up the phone and called the front desk and asked to be transferred to the manager.

Mark introduced himself, "My name is Mark Stephen and my friend Tim said to look you up. He mentioned you were friends. Could I take a couple minutes of your time to ask you a simple question?"

The meeting was set and Mark grabbed a bacon burger for lunch and went to the manager's office. Mark walked in and noticed the large mahogany desk with only a pad of paper and telephone on it. The manager set his pen down, stood up and greeted Mark and asked, "I take it you're not here to tell me the contents of The Book?" He hesitated and then added, "I won't tell a soul."

"I wish it was that easy. I mean, I wish I could just print out the ideas in The Book and give them to people but there is some work I have to do before I fully understand it."

"Am I a part of that work?"

"No, not directly. I am trying to learn some things before I can understand what The Book is saying. Let's just say I am trying to think about questions. For instance, I have been wrestling with what questions managers ask. For you, as a manager of the hotel, what questions do you constantly ask your key departments?"

"Well I haven't thought about that. I simply ask what I need to know. And I guess what I need to know about most is finances. I ask them how are they doing on their budgets or finances. That is the only question my boss asks me, so that is the question I ask them."

Talk continued for a short time but Mark had the ideas he needed and soon stood up. He shook the manager's hand and stated, "I don't want to take up much of your time. I have other meetings I need to get to and I should keep moving. Thank you for your time and I will give your regards to Tim."

Mark went out to visit other contacts Tim had supplied and to continue his quest.

I talked with several hotel managers today and all of them were interested in only one question. They wanted to know about finances because that is all their boss was interested in knowing about.

The question that a leader asks will determine the information that he or she gets. The department leaders soon realize that the only information that is relevant is about income and expenses. Soon that is all everyone focuses on and they lose out on any other relevant information. The department heads won't be interested in creativity, hospitality, opportunities or problems with people unless they affect the bottom line.

If the department heads only tell the manager what they think he wants to hear, - finances, in this case they may not tell him what he really needs to hear before it is too late. For example, the customers are not happy.

It seems obvious that just asking questions about finances is not going to tell you clearly where the organization is. What would happen if you asked different questions?

Where have we grown comfortable and how is it affecting us?

How can we do better tomorrow than we have done today?

How can we more effectively serve our customers?

Where is there a creative idea in our organization that is not being released?

September 4

The next day Mark walked into a lawyer's office. The walls were lined with books and piles of papers were stacked all over her desk. The lawyer slid her executive chair back, stood and reached out to shake hands with Mark. She stated, "If you ever need anyone to represent you, I would love to be involved. I'd do it pro bono just to help out."

"Thanks," Mark replied, "I'm hoping I don't need the help but I will keep it in mind. I won't take up much of your time as I just have a couple of ideas I am exploring and need your insight."

"All right, I will tell you what I know, but I do wish you would tell me what you know!" the lawyer replied with a smile.

"In time. I will in time. I'm exploring the area of asking questions. How do you use questions in your line of work?"

The lawyer sat down and Mark found his chair and she responded, "Now that is a difficult area. You know the old saying, 'There are always two sides to every story.'"

Mark nodded.

"Well, at a risk of being too simplistic," she continued, "we ask questions to only get one side of the story. We want things to be seen in a certain way. There are very clear laws about this but it is still the essence of our work. We know what we want our witnesses to say. We know what we don't want their witnesses to say. We are very careful about every question we ask so that the side we represent is clearest."

Mark reflected and then asked, "What is your favorite type of question?"

"The one that is probably the most useful is a question that ends with either a Yes or a No. 'Were you at this place?' 'Did you find this letter?' 'Is this your gun?' The list could go on and on but it allows no room to explain. It requires a Yes or No answer."

They talked a short while longer before Mark stood and shook her hand and left for the next appointment. Several meetings passed and Mark spent the rest of the day wandering from person to person in rainy windy weather listening to anyone who wasn't moving too fast.

I have been thinking about this whole idea of asking Yes/No questions. It is not just lawyers who ask them. We all do.

Most people ask questions that require either a Yes or No answer.

The follow up thought is this; most people don't answer the questions as they are asked. Strictly speaking, either Yes or No. They interpret what the person is asking and give them their thoughts with detail.

Mark flopped down on the bed and took a deep breath. His mind seemed jumbled. He struggled with his thoughts in a mess. After a short while he rolled off the queen bed and sat down at the antique chair by the desk in the corner. He looked out at the rain coming down and the lights of the city.

He spent the next couple of days organizing his thoughts, crumpling up papers and trying to get his thoughts as clear as he could. After much erasing and rewriting he was able to clarify his ideas.

Most questions started with:

Is, Could, Would, Should, Will, Can, Are, Am, Did, Do...

These questions end with a Yes or NO.

My thoughts on these questions are:

People are lazy and expect others to know what they mean by their questions. Did you have a good day? Which if answered should be a Yes or No. We interpret to mean how was your day and what happened in it?

<u>We are looking for certainty.</u>

Did you finish the job? You either did or you didn't. No reasons wanted, no insights into how it's going. Either it is done or it isn't. You don't have to get your hands dirty with details. Things are much easier and simpler if they are all one thing or all another.

<u>Creates polarization and extremes.</u>

Will it work? Either it does or it doesn't. You don't have to wrestle with the idea that it only works in certain contexts or with certain people.

<u>Creates boxes, definitions and judgments.</u>

Again, these questions force the answer to fit into one box or definition. Is everything in the department working well? Are we going to make budget? Will you be okay? Is this going to hurt? Did I do a good job?

<u>Produces pride, we are right, right is better.</u>

The temptation for these questions is to make the answers safe and thus the person secure. It seems like there is this struggle in most conversations to be right. To know the right thing. To say the right thing. To hear the right thing. To do the right thing.

If I am right then you must be wrong. Being right is safe, clear, secure, and protected.

Am I right to think this way?
Will other people like me?
Am I asking too many questions?

Isn't there just one right question to ask?
Do questions really matter that much?
Could I do this better?
Did I ask the right question?
Am I stupid to do this?

October 1

After different dates at a show and going to basketball games, Mark and Lynne found themselves at a table in a Chinese restaurant. Mark sat and looked over at Lynne. He looked up from his plate of sweet and sour pork and asked, "Let's see, where do we start this time? Okay, how about this, where do you think this relationship is going?"

Lynne looked down at the plate of vegetables and then looked up at Mark. She sat quietly and took a slow breath.

Mark finally blurted out, "You don't have to answer that if you don't want to!"

Lynne smiled and said, "Relax, I don't know where it is going but I do want it to continue to see what happens."

Mark looked down at his plate and took a bite of food. "Sorry about that. I asked a question and didn't give you time to answer it."

When you ask a good or hard question you have to be ready to accept silence while the other person thinks. If a good question is to provoke and create some tension and cause people to think and learn, then they need time to think. Another way of saying it is that a good question makes 'space'. Blank space within them where new thoughts, ideas or understanding can take place that they hadn't thought about in the past. This 'space' takes time to fill.

October 8

Mark lay in bed and pondered. He remembered his childhood days in school. One teacher in particular was his favorite, Miss Fritz. There was something about her that made it interesting. An idea popped into his mind. He sat up and got dressed and called his nephew's school. They agreed that he could sit in on the class to observe.

$$\bullet \quad \bullet \quad \bullet$$

Mark walked into his nephew Micah's 3rd grade class and sat down. Micah turned and waved. Mark waved back and smiled. The students sat at small desks that were all lined up in rows. There was pictures and graphs on the walls and they had settled into another day of learning.

The teacher began, "Today we are going to study Africa and the animals they have there. What would the animals of Africa sound like?"

There was a growing chorus of roars, bellows, barks, meows and everything in between. The teacher laughed and clapped her hands.

"Good, those are some of the sounds of Africa. What would you see if you were there?"

There was again a chorus of descriptions of what might be seen. This included, colors, sizes, shapes, speed and more. The teacher encouraged them and continued, "Yes, you would see some of those there. Now how about feelings you might have or what you might do if you were there?"

Again a chorus of answers rose like a symphony, "Run, I would shoot them, hide, take picture, play with them…"

"Yes, you could do most of those things. Let's look in our books and see what we can find out about these animals in Africa." The kids opened their desks and brought out their books.

Mark's mind was moving at the same speed as the kids. She asked different questions. He watched throughout the day and over and over again the teacher would ask questions that focused on different ways that the children might learn. He saw how different questions brought out different responses from different kids. Micah liked the questions about what he might see but didn't answer as many questions about feelings. Others only answered questions about feelings.

I saw the wisdom of a teacher today. She was wonderful. She asked three basic types of questions in a variety of different ways. The questions were essentially:

<u>Visual</u> – Some people see pictures, colors and think with visual words. They learn with words that have visual references. "What does it look like to you?" "What do you see as important pieces in this issue?"

<u>Hearing</u> – Some people use words and the meaning they have. They listen to what is said. They learn with words that have auditory references. "How does that sound to you?" "What do you hear that might raise questions?"

<u>Feeling or action</u> – Some people think through actions or feelings. They need their

whole body involved in order to learn. They learn with words that have feeling or action references. "How does that make you feel?" "What does that make you want to do?"

A teacher with a question is like a painter with a paintbrush. The words are the paint. The three learning styles are like primary colors.

October 19

Mark hovered over the pool table, he held the cue in his hand and eyed his next shot, "I have been thinking about this whole relationship thing, you know, with Lynne."

Tim laughed, "I know, I can see it all over you. You're still trying to figure her out. I am warning you, it will mess with your head!"

"Too late, it already has," Mark put the cue back on the wall rack and walked over and slid into the bench seat. "Sorry I don't have the heart to beat you tonight."

"You must be sick. Go ahead and talk and I will play the therapist."

"Where does the belief come from that girls won't like me? Is it just because I like computers?"

Tim rubbed his hands together and said, "Okay, let me take a shot at this. I have been thinking about this since we last talked. Your Dad was mean. Remember how you used to come over to the house when he was on a rampage?"

Mark nodded his head and Tim continued, "You told me once, all you wanted was to be loved and your Dad never told you he loved you. That much we know. Maybe you assumed that because he didn't love you, you weren't lovable?"

Mark looked up at Tim and said, "That's pretty good. Where did that come from?"

"I know, it surprised me too. Just think about it. I'm not saying anything else, as I'm sure I'll blow it. You think about it as I just gave you everything I have."

Tim stood up to leave and mumbled, "I hate to leave you like this but I did tell you earlier I have a date with a sweet little thing and I gotta go. Take care and don't let her mess with your mind. Be like me, macho man," with that Tim raised his arms out and tried to puff up his body.

Mark laughed, "Yeah, right, see ya macho man. Don't hurt yourself."

Mark sat for a while and thought. He finally got up and began to walk home.

Beliefs are formed out of my identity. Dear ol Dad planted deep in me that I was good for nothing. So how could Lynne love a good-for-nothing guy like me? The tension/ question came from how I see myself.

Could it possibly be that she doesn't see me as I see myself?
Could it be that I don't see myself as I am?

November 5

Mark threw himself into studying questions. He sat in the crowded restaurant with his pad of paper and pen next to him and slowly ate bacon and eggs, with pancakes. A Wall Street Journal was laid out in front of him on the table and he pretended to be reading it and taking notes. Mark sat there for an hour before the tables around him started to thin out. He walked down the street to a busy store and began to walk wherever there was a crowd and continued listening in on any conversation he could.

Mark then moved to a popular restaurant for lunch and sat blankly staring at his Wall Street Journal as he listened intently to any conversation going on around him. Several hours passed and the tables began to clear around him so he moved on.

The afternoon and dinner times were spent the same way. Each time he heard a question he would write it down or mark next to it if he had already written it down.

Days passed as Mark continued to listen and write down what he heard. Weeks passed and the schedule didn't change as Mark pushed himself to listen to questions and how people responded. Several yellow pads were filled with ideas as he captured conversations and the questions that formed them.

When he had enough, Mark sat at his desk and looked at his notes spread out before him, "I had no idea this would be such hard work. Over four thousand questions asked and I listened to each and every one. Why am I doing this?"

"Oops, not a good question when I am so tired. The assumption is that I shouldn't be doing this. Hmmm, What am I learning? Ah, that's better." He looked at his notes spread out before him and began organizing. He scratched out earlier ideas and tried to put them in some kind of order. He muttered out loud, "Such a simple question is so difficult to answer, 'What is a good question?'" Several days passed as Mark ordered, and reordered his ideas. Finally he was ready to write.

A good question shows you have been listening. It gives feedback that says you have understood the meaning of their words and thus a small expression of them.

A good question stimulates thinking. The better the question the more there will be a time of silence as the person thinks about a response. If you ask a good question, you also have to be comfortable with silence as the two go hand in hand.

A good question is often directed towards a specific focus. By the question you eliminate the information you don't need. A bad question is too broad and allows the person to share whatever they want about anything they want.

A good question allows the person to share what they think. A bad question is leading and hints at what the expected answer is. It says to them, "say this as this is what I want to hear".

A good question validates the other person. It says I care enough about you and what you think to ask you for your thoughts. It says to them, "you have value."

A good question <u>summons help</u>. It invites others into a deeper relationship by asking them to share what they think or feel about something.

Any question reveals as much as it asks. When I ask a question it exposes me and reveals where I am. It reveals what I am struggling with, where I need help or what interests me.

(As I write this please sense my own frustration in trying to put on paper what I am only beginning to understand as an art. It's not a paint by numbers, do it this way, technique. But a divine capacity to create and call forth life.)

December 2

Although the year was going by fast, Mark spent time each day reading, listening to others as they asked questions and listening to himself as he wrestled with his ideas. One quote from Jim Collins really stirred him. He got his pen and circled the line in the Business 2.0 magazine he was reading. He read it again out loud,

> Of all the persistently good companies we studied in Good to Great, only one was led by a CEO who had an MBA. The most common academic background, oddly enough, was law. I asked one of the CEO's how law school helped prepare him to be a business leader, and he replied, "It taught me to ask the right questions rather than come up with the right answers."[1]

He sat in his recliner and just pondered it. He spoke out his thoughts, "asking questions is key to leadership and success, yes, thank you Jim Collins for that wonderful confirmation." A call from Tim pulled him out of his apartment and down to the Billy's.

Mark slid into the booth and said, "Sorry I'm late. I got stuck in traffic."

Tim replied, "No problem. Want the latest news on your 'friend'?"

"What friend?"

"You know, the guy who paid mega-millions for what you were given."

"Oh, that friend. Anything new?"

"All we know is that he is still missing. No one has filed a missing person report or anything like that so there is no case or reason to search, but the lowdown is that people are starting to get nervous. There is one rumor he was seen in Monte Carlo drinking heavily, but that is not clear. I mean no pictures or proof for the media. This guy loved to see his picture in the paper before and now, nothing."

"I pity the poor guy. If he loves attention, then The Book will do that for him." Mark laughed out loud and continued, "He will have lots of attention, but I don't think it's the kind he wants."

Tim looked over with a frown on his face, "Ya know you're killing me. You give these little 'off the cuff' remarks about The Book and I gotta say, I'm not in the know about what you two know. I mean you want to let me in on the secret and I could enjoy it as much as you do!"

Mark settled down and replied, "Sorry, inside joke, you will be the first one in on it, just not yet. Talk to me some more about questions. For some odd reason I am fascinated with leadership and questions. Is anyone else talking about asking questions?"

"No, you gotta know asking questions isn't rated too highly. It is not one of those business skills that leaders are taught. They are told to have answers, not questions. Weak leaders are seen as the ones who have to ask questions."

They both sat quietly and finished off their drink. Mark stood up and said, "I'm sorry but I can't finish the pool championship series tonight. I have another appointment. Thanks for the thoughts though. That helps clarify some things I was wrestling with."

It seems to me, leaders deal with questions. In a sense, that is their work. Not necessarily answering them all, but knowing what are the most important ones to ask in any given situation. It seems funny to even write this, as I don't hear anyone else talking about it. Am I off the wall? Hmmm, wrong question.

Key questions for leaders might include:

What are the key decisions that I <u>must</u> be involved in?

What must happen as a result of this decision?

How did this happen?
        How was reality different from our expectations?

What do I value so highly that it must be a requirement in this decision?

On a personal note, I wonder if I react to different situations with the same old questions?

I do. I hear that small voice in the back of my mind saying, "It must be my fault. What did I do wrong this time? Why did this happen...?"

What if I changed and saw each situation as an opportunity to learn something new?

Later that week

Mark sat in his favorite chair in the magazine section at the library and read Technology Today. A particular sentence jumped out at him.

> When data has to go through a switch, half the message is lost and twice the noise is created.

Mark set the magazine down as his mind took off. Soon he realized he couldn't read anymore and put the magazine back on the shelf and headed for the door, "I wonder if that is true for people when they pass on information to others? Half the message is lost while twice the noise is created."

Three reporters tried to stop him and ask questions but Mark just ignored them and walked out the doors.

He took the long way home as he couldn't get the quote out of his mind. He called Tim and met him at Billy's.

Mark called out to Tim as he walked in and grabbed a cue, "Do you remember the old game of passing along information through a group of people? You start at one end with a statement and each person whispers to another and the last person says out loud what they heard. If you start with 'My coat is red' by the end of the time it becomes 'My boat keeper is dead'.

"Yeah, I think every kid has played that game. So what's got you all stirred up?"

"I read this quote about when data goes through a switch, half the message is lost and twice the noise is created."

"Yeah, help me here. Games, data, switches, noise, message, I can't quite see the connection."
Mark took a breath and stated, "Okay, I'm thinking about leaders, organizations and

questions. How much 'truth' does a leader really get if information has to go through three or four people before it reaches him or her? Would a leader really know what is happening at the 'front lines' if information is passed through so many people and positions?"

"I see what you are getting at. How much information is lost before it gets to a leader!"

"I was just wrestling with the idea that the questions a leader asks will determine the quality and type of information he or she gets. I had this crazy thought, it went something like this, 'an organization will only be as successful as the questions they ask and or are willing to listen to from their customers.'

"You got a year off of work and all you can think about is work? Are you feeling all right?" Tim asked.

"I am thinking about starting my own business after all of this. I wonder about the questions a leader needs to ask as the company grows? What would you think if I start a business about asking questions? I was thinking of calling the company, 'Raising Questions,'" Mark smiled as he said it.

Tim shook his head, "I think the light is on but nobody is home. Let's play some pool before you come to your senses as I want to clean your clock."

Mark grabbed his cue, "I'll show you who's home. Bring it on baby."

It seems the main difference between people who seem successful – you can define success in any way either through relationship, finances or position... - and those who aren't, is that successful people ask better questions, and as a result, they get better answers.

Where am I successful?
Where am I not successful?

[1] Business 2.0, August 2002, Article – What makes a Great Leader? By Joshua Macht, pg. 74

January 4

Mark sat reading Quinn's book[2]. He read and reread the page. It was about a consultant that was brought in on a $100 million dollar contract. There were 400 engineers about half way through a very complex project. There was a clause in the contract that said if they were too far behind it would cost them $30 million dollars as a penalty. They were very close to this and needed help. The consultant began to see what was going on and realized what needed to be done. In order help them he spent time with them and finally asked the question, "What will it take to finish this project a week early?" Those who hired him thought he was crazy but he continued working with the engineers. In the end they finished the job on time and $15 million under budget. The right question had saved the company the penalty of $30 million plus another $15 million, a total of $45 million dollars.

Mark pondered out loud, "What a brilliant idea. A question is what saved them $45 million dollars. It challenged them, allowed them to get ownership and to seek creative answers. Maybe my idea about starting a business is not so crazy after all."

Mark stood up and walked over to the kitchen table and sat down and began to write.

A question provoked them to find something they weren't looking for.

The right question, at the right time, in the right place, with the right people is one of the most powerful tools in the hand of any man, woman or God.

I was thinking of Copernicus. He asked the question, "Is our world at the center of the universe?" and it changed the way we view the heavens.

Nietzsche asked, "Is God Dead?" and it changed the way we viewed ourselves.

Hitler asked, "How superior is our race?" and demonstrated his arrogance before the world.

Mother Theresa asked, "What is the value of a soul dying in a gutter?" and we watched as she showed us.

Kennedy asked, "Ask not what your country can do for you, but what you can do for your country." and a generation was moved to action.

Martin Luther King Jr. asked, "What is the power of a dream?" and our nation was challenged to its core.

What are the questions my nation, my family or I am asking?

What's for dinner?
Who moved the cheese?
Why can't I get anything right?
How can I avoid that?
        Or
How can we work together?
How can I make the world a safer place?
What can I do to give thanks or honor others?
What can I give that will help others in need?

The quality of the questions I am asking will determine the quality of my life.

The questions that a nation asks, will
determine the quality of life of that nation.

[2] Quinn, Robert, (2000) Change the World, San Francisco: Jossey-Bass Publishers

January 26

More dates and time together form an intimate friendship for Mark and Lynne.

As they walked through the park holding hands Lynne asked, "Why are you continually interested in questions?"

Mark walked for a while. Finally he said, "I don't know what the old eccentric was trying to do but what it did in me was give me ownership of my life."

"The old eccentric, you mean The Book?"

Mark nodded, "Yeah, I've questioned things I never thought about questioning before. I can see that the questioning process for me is also an ownership process. I've taken the liberty to question my life and who I am. I have a sense of ownership in my life that I have never had before. In a sense, by asking the right questions, it has given me freedom to clarify and know what I want."

Mark pointed to a green bench that no one was sitting on and said, "Come on, I hear that is a good place to sit. Let's sit down for a while."

As they sat down Lynne asked, "What do you mean? Questions bring ownership of your life? It has always been your life, what do questions have to do with it?"

"It may have been my life, but I accepted it just as other people had defined it for me. For instance, I assumed my Dad knew what he was talking about when he called me good for nothing. Until I was ready to question that, I really had little ownership in my life. I mean what's so great about owning something that is good for nothing? In the end you only question something you care about and I can see that until I questioned my life, I really didn't care about it."

Lynne sat quietly for a few moments and then pondered out loud, "You are sometimes a very strange person. You question what others seem to take for granted and I don't know if I like that or not. I sit here and think about my life and what questions I have asked and it makes me uncomfortable and yet in a strange way I like it."

"Believe me when I say it is only recently that I have begun to do this. There are days I think I am going mad and I beat myself up. I am trying to find wisdom to know how to do it. So far it has been worth it."

They both got up off the green bench and started to walk down the path. Mark reached over and put his arm around Lynne and they walked quietly along.

The act of questioning something can be a process of taking ownership in it. If someone is not given the freedom to question, then they are not allowed the joy of ownership either.

February 14

Mark slumped in his seat as the train moved down the tracks. The slow rolling movement of it with the clickity-clack in a patterned beat lulled him closer and closer to sleep. It was a long day and weariness was winning. The sound of someone sitting down next to him stirred him awake.

He gazed over with one eye open and a serious looking man in a suit and tie sat down next to him. He peered down and noticed he was carrying a Bible. Mark slowly opened both eyes and sat up. He remembered the Gideon Bible he found at the start of the journey nine months ago.

Mark began, "I'm glad to see you. I notice you have a Bible in your hand. I found a Gideon's Bible in a hotel a short while ago and it opened up my mind to asking questions. I have been thinking about churches and the questions people ask you."

The man turned toward Mark and asked, "Yeah, what were the questions?"

"I was wondering if you and those in your congregation were removed from the community tomorrow, I mean you all just disappeared, would any of your neighbors care? I guess what I mean is, how is your community different because you are involved in it and express your concern for it during the week?"

The man sat there and seemed taken back by the question. After a moment he stated, "We are interested in saving souls, not a community." With that the man stood up as the train came to a halt and the doors opened up. He walked out quickly, seemingly glad to be gone.

I have continued to wonder about religion. I assumed there was no place for questions and that is wrong. I mean, God himself asks questions of us. Maybe questions play a role in all relationships. I'm thinking about this because I had a funny experience today.

I asked a minister today a question about how much he influenced the community he lived in. It was like I hit him. He gave me this short answer and then got off at the next stop. I was hoping to provoke him to care about the community by asking a question. I don't think he liked the idea that someone would ask such a question.

I thought it seemed a pretty good question. It would provoke me and that seemed a good thing for leaders to be provoked. However, when I asked it, he appeared to look like a man who was not used to people raising difficult or provoking questions. Like he was above being questioned since he had all the answers.

Doesn't seem like he has read the parts of his Bible where his own leader started by asking difficult questions of us.

As I have thought about it, I think I asked the question too quickly. I didn't ask lighter questions and get a chance to get to know him. I just jumped right in and was too quick to ask something that needed the protection of a relationship to allow him to receive it. I must be more careful about that in the future.

How is the community different because of my life and how I live it?

February 26

Mark jumped on the trampoline with Aimee, Micah, Markie, Matty and Katherine. They took turns being bounced high in the air as Mark's weight on the trampoline pushed them high in the air when they jumped. Between the laughter the questions continued. "Who is your girlfriend?" "Are you getting married?" "What are you doing on your vacation?" "How come you don't come over more often?"

The dinner call was given. Everyone reluctantly headed for the door and into the kitchen.

I was struck by a very challenging thought. A child is comfortable with and asks a question because they understand Dad or Mom knows the answer and because of that, they're safe. They can ask a thousand questions and not worry because it is clear that someone knows the answer even if they can't understand it yet.

Who knows the answers when we grow up?
Is that why humanity feels so insecure?
Maybe that is God's role. We can ask
questions and it is okay not to know
because we know that He does know and we
trust Him.

I don't ask the questions because I don't
know who has the answers. I have removed
God from my world and now I am insecure
because I need to have all the answers and I
know I don't.

Who is God?
Who can help me?
How can I be safe?

March 5

Tim slid into the booth and began, "They found the other guy dead." He leaned forward and continued, "A suicide note was next to him."

Mark quickly replied, "What did it say?"

"It simply said, 'I wanted answers. He gave me a question mark. I don't care about questions. It was a foolish quest and I yield to the futility of life.'"

Mark nodded his head and Tim exclaimed, "You're not surprised!"

Tim looked around and almost whispered, "I don't know what is going on but if I was you I would protect myself. We don't know if it really was a suicide note."

"Trust me, it has a ring of truth to it."

Tim exclaimed, "What do you mean? You are the only one who knows what's in The

Book. You're going to have to help me here as I don't know what you know."

Mark thought for a minute and finally said, "Okay, I think I may need to take some action to protect myself. I am going to decide on a publisher who will publish my ideas from this last year in my working with The Book. There has been lots of interest and I will ask them to publish it quickly so that I can announce The Book will be given to the Library of Congress a week after my own book is released."

"So what about me? When can I see The Book?"

Mark stood and walked over to the pool table, "The score is tied. This is the world championship. Arm yourself, as it is a dual to the finish. You win and I'll show you The Book today. You lose and you have to wait until a week before the book is published."

"You're on. I can't wait to read The Book for myself."

• • •

Mark was pleased at the loss but he didn't show it. He had a reputation to watch over. Mark called Lynne and asked her if she wanted to see The Book. She was excited and met them at the bank.

• • •

Tim reached into the safe deposit box and carefully pulled The Book out. He looked over at Mark.

Mark nodded and said, "You somehow managed to beat me. Go ahead. See the mysteries of the world. The researched wisdom of mankind that is going to save us, open it and see all that I have learned."

Lynne looked over Tim's shoulder as he opened the book and looked at the large question mark.

He slowly turned the pages and realized they were blank. He flipped through the whole book and then looked up at Mark, "You didn't change anything?"

Lynne grabbed the book and looked at it herself.

In unison they both said, "That's all there is?"

Tim stated, "You have been wresting with this over the last year…"

Lynne butted in, "asking questions…"

Tim held his hand up and declared, "That's why you have been asking questions about questions."

Mark lifted his eyebrows and stated flatly, "That's why the man killed himself. Can you imagine paying hundreds of millions for that?"

Lynne closed The Book and slid it into the safe deposit box. Mark slid up next to her and grabbed her hand and said, "I have one more question I would like to ask you."

Lynne gave a sigh and said, "Only one more question? I don't believe you."

Mark stammered, "Well… Okay. I guess I won't stop asking questions… but this question has particular importance to you and I."

Lynne stepped back with eyes wide open and Mark dropped to one knee. Both his hands gripped her left hand and he said, "The most important question I have ever asked is this next one. Will you marry me?"

Lynne squealed out loud and held her hand to her mouth and said, "Oh my," she reached down and pulled Mark to his feet and grabbed him and kissed him and finally said, "Yes, I love that question. Yes."

Tim congratulated them both and after a few minutes they all settled down. They all walked out of the vault with Mark and Lynne holding hands and looking often at each other.

Tim finally said, "I wish you would hurry up and get your book published as I can't wait to write about this."

Lynne replied, "Please don't stop asking questions. I love that about you."

Mark noticed that neither of his friends asked a question. *I wonder why*? He asked himself, then smiled.

The End of The Beginning Part 1

Appendix

As a side note, it seems to me at the end of this year that questions may run through a process. I have not known where to put it so I have put it in the back for those who might be interested. I have this funny habit of trying to organize my thoughts into patterns and this seems to be a pattern that may help some of you.

It seems to me that a good question can cause tension, or tension will bring forth a question. Either way, when there is tension it can take us deeper or we can just deal with it as a positive or negative area. It depends on us.

I trust it doesn't need much explaining as I have seen it clearly in reading and rereading the journal and trying to make sense of it all.

Tension Raises Questions

Tension	Negative	Positive
Questions	Conflict	Adaptive learning
Exposes Beliefs	Polarization (Extreme)	Self Awareness (Pain-growth)
Reveals Identity	Division (Splits)	Transformation (Synergy)
Results	Isolation (Death)	Relationships (Life)

. . .

Many people do not understand the point of tension, thinking that if there is tension, something is wrong. In order to have someone be different there must be tension, and for someone to be the same would be boring. There is a healthy tension in our relationships that we all need.

Without tension there is apathy. With too much tension there is stress. Managing tension seems the essence of life.

About the Author

Unabashed in his pointed questions and unrelenting in his encouragement for those around him to live a life of integrity, Dr. Matthew Rawlins is a passionate educator and brilliant communicator in both speech and writing. He has been invited to lecture in over 18 nations, and has published nine books. He gained his Ph.D. in Philosophy through the University of Wales, and currently serves in numerous leadership capacities within the University of the Nations. His work specifically focuses on how to talk about difficult issues that a group or team may be stuck in. Dr. Rawlins' theoretical and practical approaches to leadership development, communications, and education are applicable to almost any individual or organizational structure.

You can contact him at:
mrawlins@hawaii.rr.com